THE CURSE OF THE EGYPTIAN MUMMY

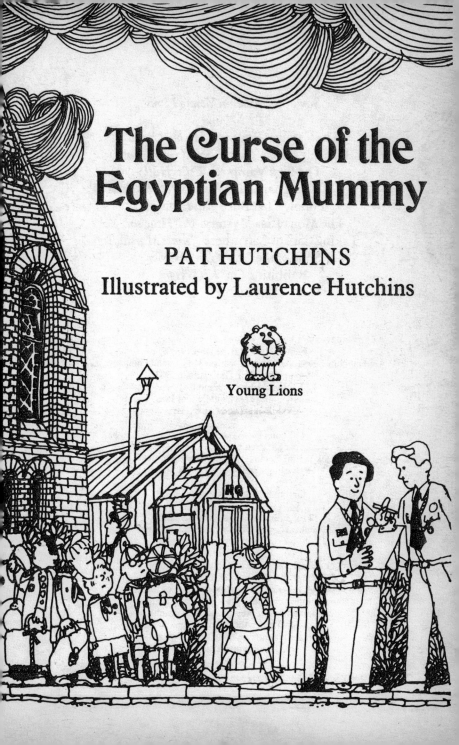

The Curse of the Egyptian Mummy

PAT HUTCHINS
Illustrated by Laurence Hutchins

Young Lions

First published in the USA 1983 by
Greenwillow Books, a division of William Morrow and Company, Inc.
First published in Great Britain 1983
by The Bodley Head Ltd
First published in Young Lions 1985
Eighth impression April 1990

Young Lions is an imprint of
the Children's Division, part of
the Collins Publishing Group,
8 Grafton Street, London W1X 3LA

Printed and bound in Great Britain by
William Collins Sons & Co. Ltd, Glasgow

For
Roger Ruse,
Sam, Peter, Nathan,
Victoria, Daniel, Jenny, David
and all the Fifteenth Hampstead Cubs

Contents

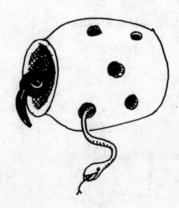

1
The News Flash

The heavy grey clouds rolled across the sky as the 15th Hampstead Cub Scouts started arriving at their headquarters.

Akela, the Cub leader, and Skip, his assistant, were checking the Cubs' names against the list in Akela's hand while the boys piled their rucksacks into the bus parked outside the headquarters.

"Oh, no!" groaned Skip, running his eyes down the list and spotting the twins' names. "Are they both coming?"

Akela nodded, just as the twins came hurtling down the High Street, scattering shoppers in every direction.

A fat drop of rain bounced off Skip's nose as he saw the twins grab Peter's and Sam's caps and throw them into the air. He sighed heavily. "And rain into the bargain," he muttered.

Akela glanced up at the sky. "I think it's just a shower," he said cheerfully. "I'm sure the weather will brighten up for the weekend."

Skip sighed again as the twins turned their attention to Nathan. "I bet it doesn't. It always rains when we go camping. It rained every single day last time."

"Still, we enjoyed ourselves just the same," Akela replied, "in spite of getting a bit wet."

"A bit wet!" Skip repeated. "We were almost drowned!"

"Only Albert," Akela corrected him, "and that wouldn't have happened if someone hadn't loosened his tent pegs."

He gazed thoughtfully at the twins, who were throwing Nathan's cap to each other while Nathan jumped up and down trying to catch it.

"And we did find him," he continued, "although it's just as well his sleeping bag got caught on the tree before he reached the stream. Still," he added brightly, "I'm sure he would have floated."

"He'd have had to," Skip murmured. "He couldn't swim."

"At least he slept through it," Akela said.

"Which is more than the rest of us did," Skip finished.

"And this time," said Akela, trying to cheer up Skip, "Mr and Mrs Webb are the helpers."

"Oh, good!" said Skip, brightening at the thought of the delicious steak and kidney puddings that Mr Webb made. "They're very good cooks."

Sam and Peter, who had wandered over to Akela to get away from the twins, overheard Akela.

"Great!" said Sam, turning to Peter. "Mr and Mrs Webb are helpers. They make smashing hamburgers."

"Is Victoria coming too?" Peter asked, looking around for her. Victoria was in their class at school.

"She's already at the campsite with her parents," Akela replied. "They went this morning to get in the provisions. Ah, good!" he exclaimed, seeing two figures struggling towards them. "Here comes Albert."

"Goodness," Skip murmured, as Albert, bent double under the weight of his rucksack, was knocked from behind by the huge suitcase his mother was carrying, making the plastic bag with his best suit in it slide down under his feet.

"Crikey! He's exploded!" one of the younger Cubs shouted, as pots, pans, brushes, and several pairs of clean underpants burst out of Albert's rucksack as he fell.

The Cubs crowded round him with interest.

"Oh, dear!" said Akela, rushing over to Albert, and looking down at his scowling face. "Are you all right?"

"You silly boy!" Albert's mother cried, before he had time to open his mouth. She pulled the plastic bag from under his feet.

"It's not funny," she snapped at the twins. "I've only just washed his uniform." She turned to Akela. "Trust him to find the only puddle in Hampstead to fall into. And don't just lie there," she went on, poking Albert with the coat hanger. "Get up."

"I can't," gasped Albert.

"I think we'd better help him," said Akela, surprised at how heavy the rucksack still was as he lifted it off Albert's back.

The rest of the Cubs (apart from the twins, who had discovered a tube of toothpaste and were taking turns squirting it at everyone) helped collect Albert's belongings. Albert, having staggered to his feet, was being dabbed at with a lace handkerchief by his mother in a vain attempt to clean him up.

"Now that we're all here I'll get the engine warmed up," said Skip, climbing on to the bus just as

Albert's mother, having given strict instructions to Akela concerning Albert's bedtime, was about to give strict instructions to Skip concerning driving a bus.

"Now make sure you brush your teeth three times a day," said Albert's mother, as Albert stepped on to the bus.

"And mind you brush your hair too," she warned, as Sam and Peter edged past Albert, who was blocking the doorway.

"And be sure to wash behind your ears!" she

cried, as the twins pushed past Albert.

"And don't forget to wear clean underpants every day!" she shouted, as Nathan and the rest of the Cubs piled on to the bus.

"You never know when you might land up in hospital!" she yelled, as Akela said good-bye politely and closed the door. He didn't seem to notice her tapping on the window and mouthing even more instructions at Albert through the glass.

"Just think," he murmured, with a gentle smile on his face, "two days of peace and quiet in the countryside. And the sun's coming out," he added dreamily.

But the boys were making so much noise as they launched into their rousing pack song, no one heard him.

"Boomalacka, boomalacka, bow wow wow
Chingalacka, chingalacka, chow chow chow
Boomalacka, chingalacka, who are we?
HAMPSTEAD CUB SCOUTS,
CAN'T YOU SEE?"

Skip groaned and tried to cover his ears, which is a difficult thing to do when you're driving.

By the time they were nearing the Cub campsite and the boys had sung every Cub song they knew, several times over, Skip couldn't stand it any more. He switched on the radio to try and drown out the noise.

"Hey! Listen to this!" he shouted, turning up the radio.

The unexpected volume silenced even the twins.

"We repeat our special news flash," the voice crackled through the bus. "Police in Buckingham-shire are puzzled by the discovery of an unidentified body found in the village of Middle Claydon."

"Crikey!" whispered Sam, nudging Peter and Nathan. "That's where we're going!"

"The police," the voice continued, "are searching for a snake in the village, as the man appears to be the victim of a deadly snake bite."

2
Snakes Alive?

The boys were in a fever of excitement at the news, and lost all interest in singing. Although the campsite was a few miles outside Middle Claydon, they persuaded Skip and Akela to stop in the village by saying they wanted to use the public lavatory there. (Although they were really hoping to find the snake, or better still, another body.)

Akela and Skip agreed, as they were very curious now too, and anyway, they'd made good time, and there would be plenty of light left to get the tents up.

"It must have escaped from a zoo," said Akela, as the children interrupted each other with blood-curdling tales of poisonous snakes, making some of the smaller boys, who hadn't been camping before, begin to wish they'd stayed at home.

"There aren't any venomous snakes in Buckinghamshire," he added, gently shaking Nathan, who appeared to be slipping into a trance as Peter, impersonating a rattlesnake about to strike its victim, gazed deeply into his eyes, trying to hypnotize him.

"It probably escaped from Hallworth Park," Skip said. "They have a zoo there, and it's only a few miles from Middle Claydon. Knowing our luck," he muttered, switching off the radio after hearing the weather forecaster predict rain, "it's probably making its way to the campsite now."

"I'm quite sure they will have caught it by now," Akela said.

"I wish I was sure," Skip murmured, frowning into the rear view mirror which Albert had obstructed by leaping from his seat.

"It got me!" gasped Albert, as the tiny droplets which followed the sharp hissing sound hit the back of his neck.

"It struck from behind," he groaned, and turning his head, he saw one of the twins, who were sitting

behind him, vigorously shaking an unopened can of Coca-Cola, while the other gazed back at him innocently, with the ring from his opened can (which was in direct line with Albert's neck) still on his finger.

"I'd rather you didn't do that in the bus, boys," said Akela. "It makes the seats horribly sticky."

Albert scowled at the twins, wiped the Coca-Cola

spray from his neck, and sat down again, as Skip steered the bus towards the village.

Quite a few cars were converging on the village, as the drivers heard the report in their cars and wanted to join in the snake hunt. A police van with a loudspeaker on top was parked in the centre of the village, warning people about the snake, and groups of people stood around the van, talking excitedly.

"They haven't found it yet," said Sam with satisfaction, listening to the loudspeaker as the Cubs piled off the bus. "Couldn't we help look for it?" he asked Akela.

"Definitely not," said Akela firmly, as the rest of the Cubs crowded round him, waiting for his answer. "It's far too dangerous."

"But we got our explorer badges last year," Sam protested. "We're used to searching for tracks."

He looked longingly at the policemen who were on their hands and knees, crawling round the village green.

The twins, seeing the protruding backsides of the

policemen, had pulled elastic bands from their pockets. Using them as catapults (and sweet wrappers as ammunition), they took careful aim.

The biggest policeman sat up suddenly, then noticing the group of Cubs, got to his feet, rubbing his bottom.

Skip, who had parked the bus rather badly, climbed on to it again, and the twins, looking innocently up at the sky, stuffed the elastic bands back into their pockets, as their target advanced towards them.

"May I suggest, sir," said the policeman, addressing Akela, but eyeing the twins suspiciously, "that you move on as quickly as possible. We're still searching for the poisonous snake, and we wouldn't want any of these little chaps harmed now, would we, sir?" His eyes glittered as he continued to gaze at the twins.

"Goodness me, no!" said Akela, noticing the glint in the policeman's eyes, and taking a nervous step backwards.

"But we could help!" Sam insisted. "We've got our explorer badges. Our green ones," he added proudly, pointing to a badge on his sleeve. "And we did some tracking for that. We've tracked rabbits, squirrels, stoats, even a badger."

"Ah! But you've never tracked a poisonous snake though, have you, sonny?" said the policeman, taking his eyes off the twins, which was a mistake, and wagging his finger at Sam.

"We've never had the chance before," said Nathan.

"There aren't any poisonous snakes in Buckinghamshire," Akela explained stiffly, "but if there were, I'm quite sure my boys would spot their tracks."

"Ah, well," said the policeman, not noticing the twins shaking the can of Coca-Cola behind him, "I've seen what the little devils can do!"

"Do they rattle before they strike?" asked Peter in awe.

"Some do, some don't," said the policeman, as the

twins rattled the ring opener against the can.

"And do they hiss, too?" asked Nathan, wide-eyed, just as the twins pulled the ring from the can.

The policeman clutched his neck as the hissing Coca-Cola spray hit it, spun round, and saw the twins with their opened can.

"Would you like a sip, sir?" the twins asked sweetly.

"As I was saying," said the policeman through clenched teeth, "you'd better be on your way. We've found one body already." He fixed his narrowed eyes firmly on the twins. "WE DON'T WANT TWO MORE ON OUR HANDS!" he roared.

"Of course," said Akela, taking another step backwards as the policeman stalked off towards the road.

"Can we help you across, sir?" the twins shouted.

"I think he can manage on his own, boys," said Akela, hoping he'd misheard the policeman's reply. "Now, boys, you heard what he said. Those of you who want to use the toilets, go now. I want you all back on the bus in five minutes."

"I'd better go with them," said Skip, who had rejoined them when he'd realized that the policeman wasn't interested in his bad parking, "and try and keep an eye on those twins."

The smaller Cubs, who didn't dare go on their own in case the snake was lurking in the toilets, trailed after Skip. Akela attempted to count the rest of the boys who were climbing on to the bus.

"You never know," said Sam to Nathan and Peter as they stepped on to the bus. "It might be at the campsite by now. It's only two miles away."

Akela, noticing the empty Coca-Cola can lying in

the aisle and hoping to change the subject, asked Sam to put it in the rubbish basket outside. Skip appeared with the twins and the smaller Cubs as Sam jumped off the bus, but Albert wasn't with them.

"Look!" shouted Sam, dropping the empty can into the rubbish basket and lifting something out of it, just as Albert (who was tripping over his feet, as someone had tied his shoelaces together) appeared.

Sam ran back to the bus. The children crowded round him, hoping it was a snake.

"I found it in the rubbish basket," said Sam.

"What is it?" asked Peter in a disappointed voice, looking at the black statue.

"It looks like an ibis," said Akela, beckoning to Albert to hurry up.

"Oh, no!" said Skip, looking at the bird. "Guess what! We've forgotten our owl mascot."

"Well," said Akela, "this might not be an owl, but it is a bird. It will do as a substitute mascot."

Skip closed the door after Albert had staggered through it, and Akela did another quick count. "Good," he said, "we're all here. We can go now."

And as the bus pulled slowly away from the village, none of them noticed a big man searching desperately in the rubbish basket, and then gazing intently at the departing bus.

3
The Ghost

"Here we are," said Akela, as the bus bumped along a little country lane. "A perfect evening," he added, trying to put all uneasy thoughts out of his mind (which was difficult, as the boys, having lost interest in the statue, were talking about poisonous snakes again).

"It won't last," said Skip, who was the only person listening to Akela. "The weather forecast says rain."

He turned the bus into the driveway that led to the campsite.

"You can bet the heavens will open just as we're putting the tents up," he added, switching the engine off as they reached the sheds that served as kitchen and bathrooms.

"I can just see it," he predicted darkly, "battling against gale force winds and torrential rain." He shook his head. "And knowing our luck, poisonous snakes as well." He sighed as he opened the door.

The Cubs, who couldn't wait to tell Mr and Mrs Webb and Victoria about the snake, scrambled out of the bus, jostling one another in the rush to get to them; while Mr and Mrs Webb and Victoria, who couldn't wait to tell Skip, Akela, and the Cubs about the snake, scrambled out of the kitchen, jostling one another in the rush to get to them.

"Have you heard about the snake?" Victoria yelled as she ran towards them. "The police suspect it escaped from a zoo," she added, ignoring the chorus of Yes.

"It has claimed one victim already," she continued

breathlessly, quoting from the latest radio announcement.

"The police are making extensive inquiries," she finished importantly.

"We know," muttered Peter, "we saw them."

"Isn't it dreadful?" said Mrs Webb, when she could get a word in edgeways. "And nobody seems to know anything about the poor man who was bitten." She glanced at Victoria, who was busy trying to organize a snake hunt.

"Victoria seems convinced that the snake has made its way to the campsite," she added, laughing nervously. "She's been looking for it ever since we heard the news on the radio."

"Impossible," said Mr Webb, laughing rather nervously too. "Middle Claydon is over two miles away. It could never get this far."

"No, of course it couldn't," Akela agreed, still feeling uneasy as he watched the younger Cubs move well away from the grass, while the others poked about in it.

Sam, who was still holding the statue and wanted to join in the search too, looked for somewhere to put it, then, spotting a hole in a hollow tree, set the bird inside.

"Those boys should be helping to put up the tents," said Skip, "not searching for snakes. The weather forecast did say rain," he reminded Akela, frowning at a tiny white cloud that flitted across the blue sky.

"We'll finish preparing supper while you put them up," said Mrs Webb. "I'm afraid we've got a little behind with all the excitement."

"There's a choice of hamburgers and french fries," said Mr Webb, watching in fascination as the twins wiggled the length of rope they'd found across the grass towards Albert.

"And snake and kidney pudding. I mean steak and kidney pudding," he corrected himself hastily. He smiled weakly at his wife. "Let's go and put the vegetables on."

It didn't take long to put up the tents, considering the time it took to release Albert, who, the twins said, had accidentally got caught up in the ropes, and, of course, the time the children took looking for snakes.

Victoria had insisted on helping Sam, even though he told her he didn't need her as Peter and Nathan, who were to share the tent with him, were helping already.

The steak and kidney pudding and the hamburgers and french fries were delicious. As it was a warm evening they ate outside, and apart from the worm which mysteriously appeared on Albert's plate, the supper was most enjoyable. The twins, who were sitting next to Albert, seemed terribly shocked when they pointed the worm out to him.

Victoria tried to get Sam, Nathan, and Peter organized into another snake hunt, but they lost interest when Akela suggested they light the campfire after they'd done the washing up. In fact all the children seemed to forget about the snake as they crowded round the blazing campfire that Akela had lit by the edge of the woods.

Mr and Mrs Webb, who enjoyed a good sing-song, joined them.

"Well," said Akela contentedly, when they'd sung themselves hoarse, "it didn't rain after all." He smiled up at the stars that were beginning to appear.

"You can never trust the weather forecast," Skip complained, trying to keep track of the twins, who kept disappearing into the darkness, then re-appearing unexpectedly, frightening the younger Cubs.

"I think it's time for a ghost story," said Akela. "You can't sit round a campfire and not have a ghost story," he added, as the children cheered (although some of the younger Cubs' cheers sounded a bit half-hearted).

"And you can't sit round a campfire and not toast marshmallows," said Mrs Webb. The children cheered again.

"I'll go and get them from the kitchen." And as Mrs Webb stood up, the children held their breath, waiting for Akela to begin.

"The lonely owl's eerie cry echoed across the dark woods," Akela began in a trembling voice.

"Oh, no," groaned Skip, "not that one again."

"The lonely owl's eerie cry echoed across the dark woods," Akela repeated, ignoring Skip. He stopped, as an owl call echoed across the woods.

The younger Cubs grabbed each other in alarm, and even Mrs Webb, who had started walking towards the kitchen, paused, then shook her head before continuing.

"I think the owl must have heard your story before, too," said Mr Webb.

"To-wit, to-woo," Akela continued defiantly, glancing at the woods, half expecting another inter-ruption. He lowered his voice. "The owl was the only one that had seen the ghostly white shape that flitted between the trees," he hissed.

Victoria, who had perched herself next to Sam, fell off the log as she grabbed his arm. "No, he wasn't," she whispered, her eyes wide with horror as she pointed to the woods.

"C-crikey!" stuttered Sam, shaking Nathan, who was sitting next to him.

"The ghostly apparition seemed to melt away," Akela went on, as Nathan shook Peter and the four children gazed spellbound at the ghostly apparition that seemed to be melting into the trees.

Victoria was the first to come out of the trance.

"Look!" she shrieked, jumping up and making the rest of the children fall off the logs too. "A ghost!"

Everyone fell silent and gazed at the woods.

But the shape had vanished into the darkness.

Akela opened his mouth to speak.

It was Mrs Webb's cry of alarm that stopped him.

4
Suspects!

"The tents!" Mrs Webb cried, as she stumbled towards them. "Someone's been at the tents. They're in a dreadful mess! Someone," she added breathlessly, "has ransacked them!"

The children, who had been gazing at Victoria in alarm, looked even more alarmed as they gazed up at Mrs Webb.

"Good heavens," exclaimed Akela, jumping up and pulling a flashlight from his pocket. "We'd better go and investigate."

Skip and Mr Webb jumped up too.

"What about our ghost?" Victoria demanded, as they raced towards the tents. "We saw a ghost," she told her mother, who was looking blankly at her.

"It was probably a shadow you saw," Akela shouted.

"It can't have been a shadow," Sam called after Akela. "I saw it too. It was white."

Mr Webb glanced over his shoulder at Sam. "Maybe it was a patch of mist."

"No, it wasn't," Peter cried. "I saw it too."

"So did I," Nathan yelled.

The rest of the children, realizing that Mrs Webb was heading back towards the tents too, decided it was safer to stick with the adults and were chasing after the beam of light from Akela's torch.

"I don't think they believe us," said Victoria indignantly, keeping close to Peter and Nathan as they followed Sam through the darkness towards the lighted kitchen which illuminated the row of tents.

They gasped when they saw the tents, and ran to join the rest of the children who were standing with Mrs Webb staring in disbelief at the clothes, books, toilet articles, and empty rucksacks that were strewn around the entrances of the tents.

Akela, Skip, and Mr Webb were walking along the

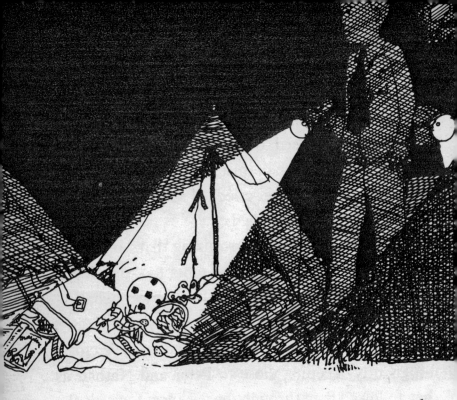

row in grim silence, beaming their torches at the mess inside. They stopped beside the children.

"Whoever could have made this mess?" said Akela wearily.

"I'd like to get my hands on the person or persons who did," Skip muttered, eyeing the twins.

Akela glanced at the twins — it seemed everyone was looking at them.

40

"None of my Cubs would do anything like this,"
he said firmly. "Would you, boys?"

They all shook their heads.

"Whoever it was," said Mrs Webb, "must have
been interrupted when I switched on the kitchen
light. I thought I heard a noise —" she frowned—
"but I'm afraid I didn't actually see anyone."

"I bet it was the ghost," Victoria shouted. "I've

heard of ghosts that throw things about. Polter-ghosts, or something."

"But the ghost, I mean the white figure," Peter added hastily, "was in the woods."

"And we saw it when your mother went to get the marshmallows," said Sam. "It can't have been in two places at once."

"I suppose it could have been a fox or a badger," Akela said doubtfully. "They're very intelligent animals. I remember one year we were camping in Wales a badger managed to get through the screen door and open the food cupboard in the kitchen."

"Well, this badger must be a mathematical genius," said Skip, beaming his torch into the tent that Albert shared with the twins, "because he managed to work the combination lock on Albert's case."

Everyone stared at the suitcase which was lying on its side. All Albert's clothes, which had been so neatly pressed and folded, lay in a crumpled heap in front of the tent, the contents of his rucksack scattered on top of it.

"I had written the numbers on the side of the case," Albert admitted, "so I wouldn't forget the combination. Quite small," he added, as Skip gave him a funny look.

"Maybe it was the police," said Sam, "looking for the snake."

The rest of the children, who had forgotten all about the snake in the excitement, huddled closer together, peering anxiously at the ground.

"I suppose it could have been," Akela said uncertainly.

"But surely the police would have told us they were here," said Mr Webb. He shook his head. "No, I don't think it could have been the police."

"So the list of suspects is down to two," said Skip, looking at Victoria. "A ghost that can be in two places at once, or—" he turned to Albert—"a badger with very good eyesight."

"Why?" asked Albert, looking puzzled.

"So he could read the combination written on the side of your case," Skip replied.

"Oh," said Albert, looking even more puzzled.

"Well," said Akela, as some of the younger Cubs, who were rather over-excited, started saying they wanted to go home, "it's no good standing around making wild guesses. Let's get the tents tidied up and see if anything is missing."

So while Skip and Akela and the bigger children sorted through the mess, Mr and Mrs Webb calmed down the smaller boys by giving them mugs of hot chocolate with the marshmallows that were to have been toasted on the campfire floating on top.

By the time their tents were ready and they'd brushed their teeth and saluted the flag, the little ones were so tired they could hardly stand up. While the rest of the children had their hot chocolate, Mrs Webb tucked the younger Cubs into their sleeping bags, promising to keep the kitchen light on all night.

"Nothing seems to be missing," said Akela, looking round at the anxious faces. "Still," he added, "Skip and I had better take turns keeping watch tonight. Just in case."

Victoria, who had planned to move her sleeping bag into Sam, Peter, and Nathan's tent, decided she'd sleep in her parents' tent after all.

When they'd all finished their drinks and Skip had checked that the campfire was out, Akela suggested that they should forget all about snakes and ghosts and go to bed.

"I was really scared when I saw that white thing," Peter said, as he, Sam, and Nathan walked back towards their tent after brushing their teeth.

"I was scared when that owl hooted," Nathan admitted.

"Yes," said Sam. "I remember it hooted just as Mrs Webb went to get the marshmallows."

"And then we saw the ghost, I mean the white thing," Peter corrected himself, "and then Mrs Webb shouted."

"I wonder who did mess up the tents," said Nathan, noticing that the twins were unusually quiet as they followed Albert into their tent. "Do you think it was the twins? They're always up to something."

Sam frowned as they entered their tent. "I don't think so," he said, shining his flashlight into his sleeping bag to check for snakes. "I don't think even they would dare do a thing like that."

"I wonder who it was," Nathan persisted, as he and Peter checked their sleeping bags too.

"I don't know," Sam said. "It's funny," he added, as gentle plopping noises came from the canvas above them. He climbed into his sleeping bag and switched off his flashlight. "That substitute mascot doesn't seem to have brought much luck. First the tents are ransacked. Now it's raining."

5
Miss Hylyard

"A beautiful morning," Akela announced at breakfast.

The rain, that had soaked Skip while he was on guard during the night, had cleared up, and a warm sun beamed down on them.

The children, refreshed by a good night's sleep, were busy discussing the events of the previous day in between mouthfuls of sausage, bacon and eggs.

The twins, who were sitting at the end of the table next to Albert, seemed to have perked up quite a lot, especially when the little frog, which had somehow jumped on to Albert's plate, decided to jump off and startled Albert, who didn't know it was there, making him spill the tea he was drinking.

Even the little ones had brightened up as they

helped themselves to toast that Mr and Mrs Webb kept bringing from the kitchen and urging them to eat while it was hot.

Victoria and Sam, aided by Nathan and Peter, who had been trying unsuccessfully to convince Skip that they had seen a figure in the woods, turned their attention to Akela.

"Well," said Akela hesitantly, "I suppose one of Miss Hylyard's guests might have gone for a walk in the woods—" he stroked his chin—"although I doubt it."

"Who's Miss Hylyard?" Victoria asked.

"She's nice," said Sam. "She owns the land the campsite is on, but she lets us use it, doesn't she, Akela?"

"She also owns the big house over there," said Akela, nodding at Sam before pointing to a house in the distance. "Apparently, she's turned it into a guest home. It's something she always wanted to do."

"Talking of Miss Hylyard," Skip exclaimed in delight, "what a coincidence! Here she comes now."

A tiny, white-haired figure, wearing a pair of enormous wellington boots, came tripping towards them, clutching a plastic carrier bag in one hand and waving a stick in the air with the other.

"Hello," she cried. "Did you hear about the poisonous snake? Isn't it exciting?" she added, when she'd reached the table and sat down on the chair that Akela had pulled out for her.

"I wanted to come and tell you about it yesterday evening, but I thought you would have heard, and then two unexpected guests arrived and I'm afraid I just didn't have the time. I've been looking for it," she continued. "In fact we all have. It's great fun. It reminds me of the time I was in Cairo and saw children hunting asps. But between you and me," she lowered her voice and looked round at the children, "I don't really think it could have got this far. I was just trying to cheer my guests up."

"What's wrong with your guests?" Akela asked in concern, interrupting Sam, who was about to ask if they'd been searching for the snake in the tents the night before.

"Well—" Miss Hylyard sighed deeply—"I've already told them the bad news, and I'm afraid I'll have to tell you as well."

"Would you like to talk to Skip and me privately?" Akela asked, noticing that Victoria, Peter and Nathan were impatient to question her too.

"Dear me, no!" Miss Hylyard replied, looking

round at the children again. "What I have to say concerns the children as well."

"I wonder what they've been up to," Skip muttered to himself, looking at the twins, who were throwing crusts of toast at the younger Cubs.

"The children haven't been up to anything," said Miss Hylyard firmly, overhearing Skip. "I like having young people around. And my guests were really looking forward to it too. That's what makes it even worse," she added, taking a handkerchief from her pocket, and dabbing her eyes with it.

"There, there," murmured Akela, patting her shoulder. Miss Hylyard, having dabbed her eyes, blew her nose.

She accepted a cup of tea from a sympathetic Mrs Webb.

"I'm afraid," she said sadly, "that I'm going to have to sell the house and the land." She looked slowly round the campsite. "I'm afraid," she repeated, "that this will be your last year at the campsite. And the first and last year for my guests."

She set down her cup, and delved into her pocket for her handkerchief.

"They've become such good friends," she whispered, "and I don't know what on earth will happen to them. They don't have anywhere else to go. I'm afraid I didn't realize just how expensive it was to run a guest house. I can't afford to keep it going. I've already sold the paintings and other odds and ends, and most of the furniture too. There's nothing else left to sell," she explained, "and nobody wanted the house without the land. Oh, dear!" she added, blowing her nose again, "I didn't mean to burden you with all my problems, but I had to tell you."

Akela stared silently at the ground.

Victoria whispered to Sam, but Sam shook his head. It didn't seem the right time to question Miss Hylyard.

"Oh, dear," said Mrs Webb, breaking the silence, "I do wish there was some way we could help."

"Perhaps we could think of a way," said Skip, turning to Akela.

"Maybe we could put on a show or something to raise some money."

Miss Hylyard stood up, smiling bravely.

"I'm afraid, Skip," she said, "that I need an awful lot of money to keep the guest house running. Several thousands of pounds, and even then it would mean cutting back on expenditure." She shook her head. "No, I've racked my brains and there's no alternative. I have to sell up. Still," she added, sticking out her chin, "perhaps I could accept your kind offer of help. It would be wonderful," said Miss Hylyard, clapping her hands together, "if you could put on a little sing-song for my friends tonight. It would cheer them up enormously. They've been wanting to meet you all."

"We'd be delighted to, wouldn't we, children?" Akela replied, jumping up and addressing the children.

"That's wonderful," said Miss Hylyard, as the children nodded enthusiastically. "Shall we say after supper? And now I must get back and help my guests search for the snake." She waved the carrier bag. "Like a good Cub Scout, I'm always prepared."

Sam, seeing that Miss Hylyard was about to leave, rushed over to her, followed by Victoria, Nathan and Peter. "Excuse me," he said politely, "were you and your guests looking for the snake last night?"

"Why, yes," Miss Hylyard replied, "we all were."

"That's it," shouted Sam triumphantly. "We've solved the mystery! It was Miss Hylyard and her guests who were searching for the snake in the tents!"

"But, my dear," Miss Hylyard interrupted gently, "we were searching in the garden. We weren't anywhere near your tents."

6
The Broken Statue

Miss Hylyard smiled at Sam's disappointed face and pointed to his green explorer badge. "We wouldn't dream of competing with the professionals," she added.

Nathan, who was standing next to Sam, ignored Akela's polite cough. "Did any of your guests go for a walk in the woods last night?" he asked.

"Dear me," Miss Hylyard smiled again, "I doubt it very much. There's a nasty big ditch, at least two metres wide, all around the woods." She turned to Akela. "They're draining the woods, you know."

"They could have jumped it," Peter suggested, as Akela coughed again.

Miss Hylyard frowned. "Mrs Earnshaw is the most athletic of my guests. She's a wonderful rock-and-roll dancer, although lately she's been suffering somewhat from rheumatism, which has slowed her down considerably." She shook her head. "No, I'm afraid even Mrs Earnshaw wouldn't be able to manage that ditch, and, as I said, she's the most athletic of my guests. Of course she's the youngest too," she added. "She's only seventy-four."

"Miss Hylyard," Akela murmured, "has turned her house into a guest house for retired people."

"And I doubt whether Mr Smith would have wanted to go for a walk in the woods," Miss Hylyard continued, "because the poor man is confined to a wheelchair, and I don't think even his nurse, who is a remarkably large lady, could manage that ditch pushing the wheelchair. It's quite cumbersome."

She turned to Akela again. "He only arrived last night. Apparently the poor man has lost the power of speech and has to have his nurse with him at all times. She is the only one who can understand his requirements. Talking about requirements—" she smiled at the children — "I really must be getting back to my guests, they'll be wondering where I've got to. They'll be thrilled about the sing-song tonight," she finished, holding up her stick in farewell.

Akela sighed, as they watched her walk slowly back to the house. "Poor Miss Hylyard," he murmured. "It will break her heart having to sell up."

"I wish there was some way of raising the money," Skip replied, "but it would take a miracle to raise that sort of money."

Akela sighed again. "I suppose we'd better make the most of this weekend as it's our last one here. Come on, children," he added, trying to sound cheerful. "Let's forget about the unfortunate incident last night and get these breakfast things cleared away. Then we'll do our artist badges. There's clay in the riverbank, so those of you who want to make models can."

"Oh, good," said Albert, who already had his red and yellow artist badges, and hoped to get his green one as well.

The twins, who didn't have any artist badges, groaned. Sam and Nathan, who were huddled together with Peter and Victoria, still discussing Miss Hylyard's guests, were asked by Akela to go and dig some clay. By the time they came back with a bucketful, the tables had been cleared. Some of the smaller Cubs said they would rather do a drawing, but everyone else decided to make a model.

Akela suggested that they do models of birds.

The twins, who only wanted to use the clay because it was messy, made egg shapes, saying the baby birds were inside.

Sam, Nathan and Peter, who were still talking about intruders, found it difficult to concentrate, so their models of owls weren't terribly good either.

But Albert, who had discovered the statue of the ibis (which everyone else had forgotten about), did a marvellous copy of it before placing the statue back in the hollow tree, where it was partially hidden by leaves. Albert was so pleased with his copy that he

insisted on painting it black, like the statue, even though the clay hadn't dried properly.

"I think," said Akela, surveying the drawings and models that were on the table, "that we should go for a nature ramble. By the time we get back the clay will have hardened. Then Skip and I will decide who should get their artist badges."

He smiled at Albert, who blushed happily.

Victoria decided to join them on the ramble, as Mr and Mrs Webb had to go to the village for fresh provisions.

"I still think it was a ghost we saw last night," she said, trotting behind Sam, Nathan and Peter. "It was all white."

She turned to the younger Cubs who were trailing behind her with Albert. The twins had disappeared. "All white," she repeated. "Wasn't it, Sam?"

She turned to Sam again. "Oh!" she shrieked. "Look!"

The smaller Cubs stopped in their tracks.

"It's the ghost again!" Victoria whispered,

grabbing Sam's arm, as a white figure flitted through
the trees.

"There's something attached to it," said Sam.

Akela and Skip, who were striding ahead of them,
heard Victoria's cry and came rushing towards her.

"What's wrong?" asked Akela.

"There," Victoria hissed, pointing at the trees.
"The ghost!"

"That isn't a ghost, Victoria," Akela said gently. As the figure reached a clearing, silhouetted against the sky was a large shape in a white uniform, pushing a wheelchair.

"That must be Mr Smith and his nurse. Come on," he added, as the twins rejoined them. "Let's go back, the models will have dried now. And it's nearly lunchtime."

Victoria was very quiet as they walked back towards the campsite. The younger Cubs, tired from the walk, were drifting behind a bit, but Albert, who couldn't wait to see if his model had dried properly, ran towards the clearing where the tables were.

"Is it dry yet, Albert?" Akela asked, as they caught up with him. But Albert didn't reply. He was kneeling on the ground. On the table were several models, but Albert's was missing. Then they saw it — smashed into tiny pieces, on the grass.

7
Suspicions!

"Oh, dear," Akela exclaimed, bending down to help Albert pick up the bits of clay. "What a shame! It was such a good model." He paused. "The wind must have blown it off the table."

"There isn't any wind," said Skip. "It looks to me as though it was deliberately smashed."

"Who would do a thing like that?" Akela asked, as the rest of the children and Skip gazed at the twins, who appeared totally unconcerned.

"And besides," he raised his voice and directed it towards the twins, who seemed quite surprised, "I'm sure if any of my Cubs had done it they would come forward and admit it."

The twins gazed blankly at Akela.

Akela sighed. "An animal must have knocked it off if the wind didn't," he said.

"More likely two," Skip muttered. "Probably the same ones that messed the tents up," he added darkly, as the twins started pulling the younger Cubs' caps off their heads and throwing them in the air, unaware of Skip's baleful look.

"Never mind," said Akela briskly. He smiled sympathetically at Albert, who was gazing forlornly at the broken pieces he was cradling in his hands.

He patted Albert's shoulder. "We'd already decided to give you your green artist badge. It was definitely the best model, wasn't it, Skip?" Skip nodded in agreement.

"Maybe you'd like to make another one while Skip and I judge the rest of the work," Akela suggested, patting Albert's shoulder again. "Then we'll have lunch," he finished, noticing Mr and Mrs Webb pulling up in their car with a load of shopping.

"The police are still searching for the snake," said Mrs Webb, as she and Mr Webb came hurrying towards them. She glanced at the children, who crowded round her, waiting to hear the latest news from the village. "They still haven't found out the identity of the poor man who was bitten."

"The strange thing is," said Mr Webb, "that no one has reported a lost snake. They've contacted all the zoos, including the local one, and it seems none are missing. Oh! What a shame," he cried, noticing the bits of clay in Albert's hands. "How did that happen?"

"It got smashed," said Albert.

"What a pity," said Mrs Webb. "We were just admiring it before we left."

"Albert's going to make another one, aren't you, Albert?" said Akela. He raised his voice above the excited chatter. "The rest of you can help Mr and Mrs Webb prepare lunch."

Albert retrieved the statue from the hollow tree, and using the damp clay that was left in the bucket, modelled another copy of the ibis, while Skip and Akela walked round the table, judging which models

and drawings deserved badges.

Sam, Nathan and Peter, who had switched their conversation from intruders back to snakes, helped Mr and Mrs Webb peel the potatoes, while Albert, who had quickly finished his model, insisted on painting it black, like the last one.

The twins were put in charge of the sausages, as they kept throwing potatoes at the smaller Cubs who came into the kitchen to get the bread and butter.

Victoria put the tomato ketchup and salt and pepper on the table. When Skip asked if there was any mustard, she went to look for it, knowing there was a pot of very hot mustard in the kitchen. But when she did eventually find it, it was empty.

"Quiet please," said Akela, trying to get the children's attention as they sat down for lunch.

"Skip and I have awarded points for the artist badges. You all did quite well," he added uncertainly, looking at the twins' eggs, "so we decided you should all get your red badges. That's the first stage," he explained to the younger Cubs, who were cheering wildly.

"Some of you we've awarded yellow badges too," he continued. "That's the second stage. Albert, of course, did exceptionally well so we've awarded him his green badge, the final stage."

He looked at Albert, who had just taken a bite from his sausage, and was gasping for breath.

"In fact," Akela continued, as everyone admired Albert's latest model, which, gleaming with wet paint, had pride of place in the centre of the table, "this model is even better than the last one."

The younger Cubs looked at Albert in awe, expecting him to say something. But Albert, still gasping for breath, seemed much more interested in his sausages than his model as he turned them over and examined the thick yellow coating of mustard that had been hidden beneath them.

Akela, noticing Albert's crimson face, was afraid he might be embarrassing him, and turned his attention to the twins, who were sitting next to Albert, trying to stifle giggles.

"The twins' efforts were quite . . ." he coughed, searching for the right word, "interesting. So we decided they should have red badges too."

"Huh," Skip snorted. He didn't think they

deserved any badges for their eggs. Not even red ones.

"Sam, Nathan and Peter we've awarded yellow badges," Akela continued hastily. "I'm sure they'll get their green badges next time." He looked at Albert in concern, as Albert pushed aside his glass (which he'd already refilled half a dozen times), and picking up the huge jug of water, drained it.

"Albert," he said kindly, noticing that Albert had pushed his plate away too, "as you seem to have finished your lunch, why don't you go and wash the clay bucket in the stream? It clogs the sink up if it's washed in the kitchen. The rest of you can help clear the table and wash up."

Sam, seeing that the ibis Albert had copied was still on the table, picked it up, and put it back in the hollow tree where it was less likely to get knocked over. Then, as it was his turn to help with the washing up, he went into the kitchen to join Nathan and Peter, who were filling a basin with warm water.

Albert, whose face was still a bit pink, collected the bucket and turned to go to the stream. Seeing the twins studying his model, he turned round again and tucked it under his arm, even though the paint was still wet.

Victoria and the younger Cubs cleared the dirty dishes from the tables, while Skip, Akela and Mr and Mrs Webb had a cup of coffee and studied a first-aid book as Akela wanted the boys to do their first-aid badges later in the afternoon.

"Where are the twins?" Victoria demanded, as she took the dishes into the kitchen. "They haven't done anything to help."

"I bet they've gone after Albert," said Peter. "I bet they're after his model. I think they smashed the first one," he added. "They probably sneaked back when we were on the nature ramble."

Nathan nodded. "They probably messed up the tents as well," he said.

Sam shook his head and frowned. "I suppose they could have," he admitted, "but I still don't think that even the twins would dare do anything like that."

"Then who did?" Victoria asked.

Sam shook his head again. "I don't know."

They finished the washing up, then went outside to collect the empty coffee cups.

Skip was talking to Akela. "Do you think it was a good idea sending Albert to the stream?" he asked, remembering the last camp when Albert had floated away.

"I thought he was getting rather embarrassed by all the attention," Akela replied. "Anyway, he'll be all right, he has his swimming badge now."

Mr and Mrs Webb gasped.

"It looks as though he needed it," Skip murmured.

Approaching them was a small bedraggled figure covered in weeds and streaked with red clay. A bucket dangled from one hand.

"Oh, dear!" cried Akela, as Albert reached them. "Did you fall in?"

"No," said Albert, "I
didn't fall in."

The twins, who had
suddenly appeared behind
Albert, doubled up in helpless
laughter.

The rest of the children
crowded round Albert and
watched with interest as he
pulled weeds from his hair
with paint-stained fingers.

"I didn't fall in," Albert repeated, glancing mournfully at the twins, who were lying on the ground, clutching their stomachs and kicking their legs in the air. "I was pushed."

"That's it!" Skip exploded, advancing towards the twins, who jumped up in surprise. "I saw Albert take his model with him. You can guarantee that these two — not content with breaking the first model — pushed Albert into the stream and took the other one!"

"But, Skip," Albert interrupted.

"That model was covered in thick wet paint," Skip continued, not listening to Albert, who kept trying to say something. "They'd only have to touch it and they'd have black paint on their hands, and they can't have washed it off," he added, as Albert tugged at his sleeve. "Albert scrubbed his hands and they're still stained."

He turned to the twins. They were rooted to the spot, their hands behind their backs.

"Show us your hands!" he roared.

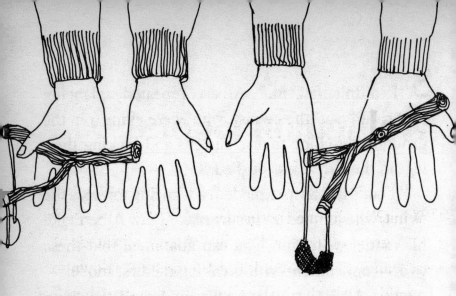

The twins thrust their arms out and reluctantly unclenched their fists.

Their hands, underneath the catapults, hadn't even a trace of black paint on them.

"I tried to tell you they didn't take it," said Albert, lifting his model out of the bucket. "They didn't push me in, either."

"Then who did?" Akela asked.

"A grown-up," Albert replied.

8
Wellington Boots!

"What?" everyone chorused.

"A grown-up pushed me in," Albert repeated. "I was leaning over the bank. I'd put my model down so I could lower the bucket into the stream, then I thought I heard a noise behind me. I thought—" he looked at the twins who were gazing at Skip reproachfully—"that someone was creeping up behind me to pinch it, so I grabbed it, and the next thing I knew, I was pushed into the stream."

"Good heavens!" exclaimed Akela. "I can't imagine anyone wanting to push a child into the stream."

"What did the person look like?" Skip demanded, noticing how the twins were now looking at him in a superior way, and thinking how easily he could imagine pushing a child into a stream.

"I don't know," said Albert. "All I saw was a great big pair of wellington boots. By the time I'd climbed out of the water, they'd disappeared."

"How strange," murmured Mrs Webb.

"There's been a lot of strange things happening," Mr Webb agreed.

"Yes," said Sam, "a man bitten by a snake in the village—"

"And then the ghost," Victoria interrupted. "Or anyway, the white thing in the woods," she corrected herself, as the twins giggled.

"Then the tents being messed up," said Nathan.

"And Albert's statue being broken," Peter added.

"It's awfully confusing," Mrs Webb said.

"I'm sure there's a logical explanation." Akela, just as confused as everyone else, sighed. "The important thing is that Albert wasn't hurt. There's no point in worrying about it, and when Albert has changed into dry clothes—" he looked at Albert, who was standing in a puddle of water—"we'll go over to the fields and do our athlete badges."

Skip, still not convinced that the twins had not had a hand in Albert's attack, grudgingly apologized to them. The rest of the children followed Albert, firing questions at him as he squelched his way to his tent, first stopping to put his model in the tree, next to the ibis, where he thought it would be safe.

The children hadn't been able to concentrate very well on the athletics that afternoon, and only Sam, Peter and Nathan, who were very good at sports, managed to get their green badges. The others managed only red ones.

Victoria beat them all and Akela said it was a pity she wasn't a Cub. But even Victoria knew she could have done better if she hadn't been thinking of other things.

They tried looking for footprints near the river on the way back, but the ground was too hard and they didn't find any.

They were still discussing Albert's attack at supper.

Akela glanced at his watch when they'd finished eating. "Six o'clock," he said. "That gives us time to fit in the first-aid badges before we go to Miss Hylyard's."

"Oh!" said Mrs Webb. "Talking of Miss Hylyard, I nearly forgot. Two of her guests came to the campsite this afternoon, poor Mr Smith and his nurse. I thought they must have wandered in by mistake as they seemed a bit startled when I came out of the kitchen to ask if they were lost, but the nurse just wanted to know if we were all going tonight."

She smiled at the children. "They must be looking forward to it very much as they seemed quite anxious that we should all go." She paused, and looked at Mr

Webb. "I said perhaps we'd stay here and keep an eye on things. I didn't mention anything about the tents, or Albert," she added. "I didn't want to alarm them."

Akela nodded sympathetically. "You were right," he said. "The last thing we want to do is frighten Miss Hylyard or her guests. They've got enough problems as it is. Still," he added, raising his voice to make himself heard above the children's chatter, "when we've finished doing the first-aid badges, we'll go and try to cheer them up." He raised his voice again, as no one seemed to have heard him. "So try not to strain your voices! We want some good singing tonight!"

After they'd cleared the tables and washed up, the children collected their first-aid kits from the tents.

Skip wanted the twins to be the patients, but as they wanted to do their badges, Victoria volunteered.

The bandaging took longer than Akela had

expected, and it was getting close to eight o'clock.

Skip was convinced that the sling that Albert had put on Victoria's arm was too tight. Victoria, who was bandaged from head to toe, agreed, but couldn't say anything as the twins, who had decided to do a full head bandage, had covered her mouth, and left only a space for her eyes and nose.

"I'll go and get the first-aid book," said Skip. "It shows the correct way to do a sling. I'm sure I left it in the kitchen."

"I'm sure you put it back in the tent," said Akela. "I'll look in the tent, while you look in the kitchen. You boys," he added, "had better make your way to Miss Hylyard's, she'll be wondering where we are. Tell her Skip and I will be along in a few minutes." He paused, as Mr and Mrs Webb came out of the kitchen.

"We've run out of milk," said Mrs Webb, "and the shops are closed. I'm sure the children will want their hot chocolate before they go to bed, so we're just popping down to the farm to get some. We'll be back in a few minutes."

"Skip and I will wait here until you get back," said Akela, as the boys packed away their first-aid kits.

"Sam, Nathan and Peter," he called over his shoulder as he went into his tent, "look after the younger boys, and stay together," he added, as the twins started to run ahead of the group. "And don't forget to tell Miss Hylyard we'll be joining you shortly."

Victoria tried to shout after the departing boys to

wait for her, but the sound was so muffled because of the bandages, they didn't hear her.

She fidgeted impatiently while Skip and Akela, who seemed to be taking ages, searched for the first-aid book. Then, seeing the boys heading towards the house without her, she jumped up and hobbled awkwardly after them.

"I've found it," Akela shouted triumphantly, coming out of the tent and waving a book in the air, just as Skip, having given up his search, came out of the kitchen.

"Oh!" Akela looked at the empty chair that Victoria had been sitting on. "Victoria must have gone with the boys. That's a pity, I'd have liked another look at that sling."

"They certainly got the bandages off a lot quicker than they got them on," Skip commented.

"Well, it was very thoughtful of them to clear them away," said Akela, as Mr and Mrs Webb returned, carrying two large jugs of milk.

"We're covered in thunderbugs," said Mrs Webb. "I'm sure there's going to be a storm."

Skip and Akela looked up at the sky. It seemed to have got dark very suddenly.

"We'd better tie the flaps on the tents," Skip remarked. "We don't want Albert floating away again!"

"I'll do them," said Mr Webb. "You'd better get going. It's past eight o'clock. Goodness," he added, looking at the empty chair. "They soon got the bandages off Victoria."

"I think they were in a hurry to get to the house." Akela laughed. "Miss Hylyard makes marvellous chocolate brownies."

And after Skip and Akela had said good-bye to Mr and Mrs Webb, they strode through the gathering darkness towards Miss Hylyard's house. They were totally unaware of the struggling, bandaged figure, which, rather rashly, had tried to take a short cut and was caught by the sling on top of a barbed wire fence.

9
"The Curse of the Mummy's Tomb"

Miss Hylyard was delighted to see the boys, and ushered them into a large, noisy room, where an ancient piano stood in a corner.

Her guests were seated in front of it. Miss Lovatt was practising on her piano accordion, and Mrs Earnshaw on her mouth organ. The rest of them were sipping glasses of ginger beer, and tapping their feet to the music.

A space had been cleared in case anyone wanted to dance, and a table was pushed against the wall, laden with plates of chocolate brownies and jugs of ginger beer.

Miss Hylyard switched the lights on as the gathering storm clouds had made the room rather gloomy.

A large grey parrot was perched on top of the chandelier. "That's Percy," said Miss Hylyard, as the children and Percy studied each other with interest.

"He should be in his cage upstairs. I don't know what's come over him. He's been such a naughty boy. He started on Friday night, making such a dreadful commotion I was afraid he would keep Mr Smith's nurse awake all night, as her room is next to mine and Percy's. I tried covering his cage with a blanket, as that usually makes him go to sleep, but he still wouldn't stop. I just had to let him out, and now he refuses to go back into the cage. Still," she added, "he enjoys a good sing-song. Now let me introduce you to my friends."

She led the children to her guests, who greeted them with equal delight, apart from poor Mr Smith of course, who, as Miss Hylyard had pointed out, had lost the power of speech.

The nurse, who had been bending over Mr Smith's wheelchair rearranging his blankets, stretched to her full height.

The children gazed up at her in astonishment as

she raised her bushy black brows and fluttered her false eyelashes at them. Her enormous face, which was framed by long blonde hair, looked like a photograph of the moon, and even the thick coating of powder she was wearing couldn't conceal the pitted skin underneath it.

Her nose, which was enormous too, had black hairs sprouting from it, and when her thick crimson lips parted in a smile, her teeth were smeared in lipstick. Her chins wobbled when she spoke.

"I do hope you are all coming," she warbled, glancing at the door.

The children, fascinated by the high-pitched voice that came from such a giant of a person, gazed at her blankly.

"I said I do hope you are all coming," she repeated, fixing her eyes on Sam, who, having heard the twins muttering something about Miss Piggy, had opened his mouth to speak.

"Oh, yes," he said quickly. "Skip and Akela will be coming in a few minutes."

"Good," the nurse murmured, patting Mr Smith's hands, which were clutching the covers. "And the nice couple who cook for you, are they coming too?"

"No, they're not," Albert interrupted. "I heard them say they would stay at the camp and keep an eye on the tents."

"What a pity," the nurse murmured. "We were looking forward to seeing them again."

"They had to stay behind," Albert continued, "because lots of funny things have been happening."

"Really?" asked the nurse sharply. "What kind of funny things?"

Sam, noticing the way Mr Smith's hands had started twitching, remembered what Akela had said about not alarming Miss Hylyard or her guests, and aimed a kick at Albert's shin.

"Well," said Albert unconcernedly, rubbing his ankle. He frowned at the twins, thinking they'd kicked him. "First of all the tents were ransacked, then my model was smashed, and then, OUCH!" Albert stopped in surprise when he saw it was Sam that had kicked him again. "I was only going to say that someone pushed me into the stream," Albert complained, as Sam attempted to indicate with a jerk of his head Mr Smith's hands, which were trembling quite violently now.

"How perfectly dreadful," cried the nurse in a horrified voice. "I do hope—" she lowered her voice — "that poor Miss Hylyard and the other dear old folk don't get to know about it." She gripped Mr Smith's small hands in her own large ones, and glanced at Miss Hylyard, who was surrounded by the rest of her guests. They were cheerfully discussing the gruesome murders in the horror film they'd seen the night before.

"The poor things would be terribly distressed," she whispered. "They have rather nervous dispositions. But what a pity about your model," she murmured sympathetically, bending towards Albert. "What sort of model was it?"

"A bird," said Albert promptly. He nodded towards Sam. "I copied it from a statue that Sam found. But I made another one," he added proudly.

"Then you must be sure to put it somewhere safe where it won't get broken," said the nurse. She turned to Sam. "I'm sure that you, sir, have put yours in a safe place."

"He has," Albert continued, "so I've put mine next to his. In the—"

"At last!" Miss Hylyard's voice rang through the room, interrupting Albert, as she ran to the door. "How lovely to see you. We thought you'd got lost!"

The children, except for the twins who were still staring, took their eyes off Mr Smith's nurse and looked at the doorway where Skip and Akela stood.

"I'm sorry we're a bit late," Akela apologized, leaning against the door to close it. "The wind is really blowing up. We had quite a battle getting here," he added breathlessly, as the lights flickered. "There's definitely a storm brewing." He looked round the room and frowned. "Isn't there someone missing?" he asked.

But he didn't get a reply. For at that moment the room plunged into darkness and the door burst open.

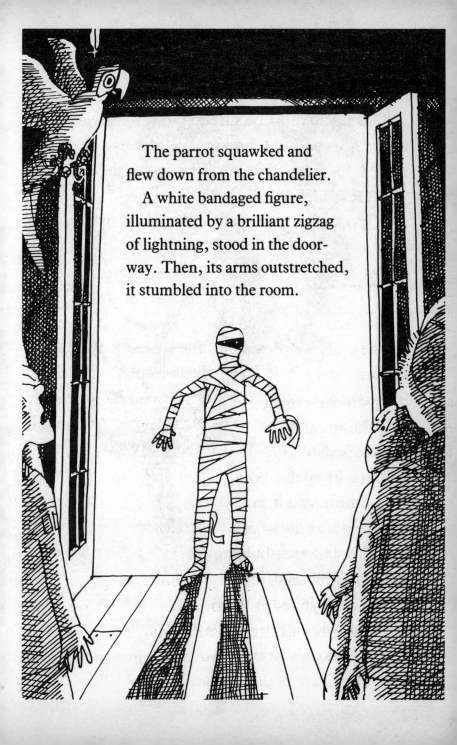

The parrot squawked and
flew down from the chandelier.

A white bandaged figure,
illuminated by a brilliant zigzag
of lightning, stood in the doorway. Then, its arms outstretched,
it stumbled into the room.

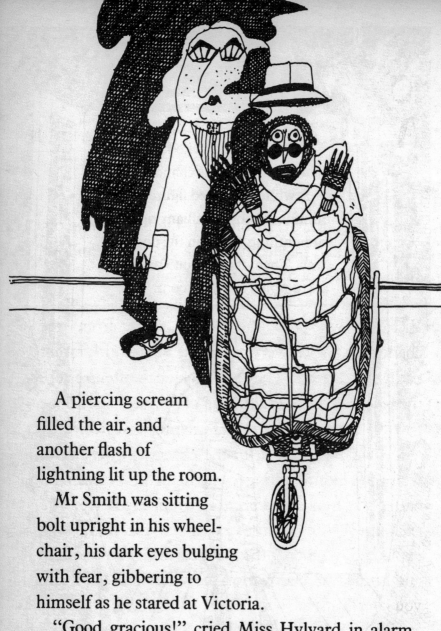

A piercing scream
filled the air, and
another flash of
lightning lit up the room.

Mr Smith was sitting
bolt upright in his wheelchair, his dark eyes bulging
with fear, gibbering to
himself as he stared at Victoria.

"Good gracious!" cried Miss Hylyard in alarm,
grabbing Akela's sleeve. "Mr Smith just spoke! He
said, 'The Curse of the Mummy's Tomb!'"

10
A Miracle

Everyone stared at Mr Smith as the lights came on. The nurse had pushed him back against the pillows and covered him up with the blanket.

"It's a miracle!" she exclaimed, glancing at Victoria, who, in the bright light from the chandelier, looked very much like a small girl, rather badly bandaged. "They say shock can often restore the power of speech, although of course," she added hastily, "the poor man can't form proper words yet."

She held tightly on to the covers, as Mr Smith seemed to be attempting to tear them off. "I think I'd better take him upstairs and give him a sedative. The excitement was a little too much for him," she explained, wrapping the blankets firmly around him and lifting him bodily from the wheelchair. "I'll join you later."

The children watched in awe as the nurse slung the struggling man over her shoulder and carried him out of the room. "The poor man can't walk, either," she called over her shoulder. The sound of struggling continued, until they heard a door slam above them. Then they heard a thump and silence.

"The sedative must have worked," said Akela, noticing that Miss Hylyard was frowning as she absently stroked Percy's ruffled feathers.

Akela could hardly hear Miss Hylyard's reply, as the guests and the children, except for Victoria, whose mouth was still bandaged, were all talking excitedly.

"How strange," she said softly. "I'm convinced he said, 'The Curse of the Mummy's Tomb.' I know a smattering of several languages," she explained, "as my father and I travelled extensively." She frowned again. "Perhaps poor Mr Smith travelled extensively too, before his illness, because I'm practically certain he was speaking in Arabic." She shook her head. "Poor man." She sighed. "He must have had a brainstorm."

Victoria, who had been standing in front of Sam, Nathan and Peter, gesticulating wildly with her arms in a vain attempt to get them to untie her bandages, hobbled over to Skip and Akela as the boys were so busy talking they didn't seem to notice her.

"Oh, dear," said Akela, turning round as Victoria thumped him on his shoulder with her bandaged arm. "We thought you'd gone with the boys. Where were you?"

"I think," Skip said, undoing the pins that secured the bandages round Victoria's head, "that we need to restore Victoria's power of speech too, before she can answer that one."

"I," said Victoria indignantly, as the bandages fell away, "got caught by Albert's sling trying to get here. It's not funny," she added, glowering at the twins.

"A pity," Akela murmured. "I would have liked another look at it."

"Well," said Victoria, "I know where it is if you want to see it. It's a good job I managed to wriggle free," she continued bitterly, "or I'd still be stuck on the barbed wire fence with it."

"Never mind," said Akela cheerfully, helping Skip to undo the rest of the bandages. "Just think, if you hadn't made such a dramatic entrance, poor Mr Smith might never have spoken again."

"That's right," Miss Hylyard agreed. "As Mr

Smith's nurse said, it was a miracle." She sighed and looked at her guests who were talking happily to the younger Cubs. "It's a pity we can't work another one," she added wistfully, "and not have to sell the house." She sighed again, as Akela patted her shoulder.

Then, noticing the way the boys were drifting towards the chocolate brownies, she smiled. "I think the children must be ready for a little refreshment," she said, "and then we'll have a good old rousing sing-song."

The children enjoyed the refreshments and talking to Miss Hylyard's guests, particularly Mrs Earnshaw, who used to work in a circus. She told them about the knife thrower, who, it was discovered when it was too late, had been prescribed glasses by his optician. He thought it would ruin his act if he wore them, but, as Mrs Earnshaw pointed out, he'd ruined his act by not wearing them.

Even the twins behaved themselves, and listened attentively when Miss Hylyard insisted that Mrs

Earnshaw tell them about the fire-eater who developed hiccups.

By the time Mr Smith's nurse reappeared, saying that Mr Smith was sleeping like a baby and the singing would not disturb him, they'd all finished eating.

Miss Hylyard settled herself at the piano, and Percy settled himself on the lid.

The nurse seemed to take a particular liking to Albert, to the twins' amusement, and patted the seat next to hers for him to sit on. But as the rest of the children were forming a semicircle round the piano, Albert managed to escape her attentions by joining them.

Miss Hylyard, who knew all the Cub songs, struck a chord on the piano, Miss Lovatt picked up the tune on her piano accordion, and Mrs Earnshaw joined in with her mouth organ. Then the children started singing, their voices drowning out the sound of the rain beating against the windows.

When they'd finished and the applause had died down, Miss Hylyard handed out song sheets, then sat down to play a medley of old songs which everyone joined in. It wasn't until the last chorus of "She'll Be Coming Round the Mountain" had faded away that they heard the pounding on the door.

Percy, who had been strutting up and down the piano, enjoying the music, squawked, and flew back up to the chandelier as the door opened.

"Hello, Officers!" Miss Hylyard called cheerfully. "Come in. You're soaking wet."

"It's the policemen who were looking for the snake in the village," Sam whispered to Peter.

The twins, recognizing the fat policeman, ducked behind the piano.

"Why do you think they've come here?" asked Peter.

The large policeman spoke, answering Peter's question. "We were just going home on our bikes," he explained. "We noticed one of the electricity pylons had been knocked down in the storm, so we thought we'd better check that your electricity was still working."

The nurse, who had seemed surprised at the sudden intrusion and had jumped up, sat down again.

"Well," said Miss Hylyard briskly, "you must get out of those wet uniforms. You can't possibly cycle home in them. You'll catch your death of colds." She smiled at two of her guests. "Mr Jones and Mr Underwood have clothes that will fit you. I'm quite sure they won't mind your borrowing them," she added, as Mr Jones and Mr Underwood smiled and shook their heads.

"Well, if you are quite sure it's not too much bother," said the smaller policeman, looking at the puddle he was standing in. "I must admit I wouldn't mind changing into some dry clothes."

The nurse, who seemed to have recovered her composure, insisted on putting their uniforms in the dryer, and as the policemen were off duty the next day, they agreed, saying that they'd collect them in the morning, not too early, as it was Sunday and they liked a lie-in.

Then, having changed and answered everybody's questions about the snake, which they still hadn't found, they said good night and left.

Akela glanced at his watch.

"Goodness me! It's nine-thirty already," he exclaimed, turning to Skip, who had been keeping an eye on the twins while the policemen were there. "We'd better get these children back to camp."

Skip glanced down at the open sandals he was

wearing and frowned. "I should have known it would rain," he muttered. "It always does when I wear these things."

Miss Hylyard smiled. "There's lots of wellingtons in the hall," she said. "Borrow a pair. We share everything here," she added.

Akela attempted to round up the children, who were saying good night to the guests. "Come along, Albert," he said, interrupting the conversation that the nurse had just started with Albert. "We don't want to forget any of you."

Albert edged away from the nurse to join the rest of the children, after quickly saying good-bye.

The nurse looked very disappointed.

Skip had already set off with the twins and the younger Cubs. Miss Hylyard led the rest of them out of the house, thanked them for coming, wished them good night, and closed the door.

Sam glanced up idly at a lighted bedroom window. A figure darted behind a curtain, and the light went out.

"Crikey!" he whispered, clutching Nathan's and Peter's arms.

"What is it?" demanded Victoria, who was standing behind them.

"Mr Smith," Sam breathed, "and he was walking."

11
More Suspicions

"Akela!" hissed Nathan, tugging at Akela's sleeve. "Sam has just seen Mr Smith."

"That's nice," murmured Akela.

"But he was walking," Sam shouted, pointing up to the darkened window, "and the nurse said he couldn't."

"That really is remarkable," Akela exclaimed. "He must have made a complete recovery. He's obviously regained the use of his legs, as well as his voice. It must have been the shock of seeing Victoria bandaged from head to toe." He frowned thoughtfully. "Perhaps the poor man saw the film 'The Curse of the Mummy's Tomb' when he was a child." He shook his head. "It must have had a profound effect on him."

"If he couldn't walk before," said Victoria, "why was he wearing shoes?"

"I didn't know he was wearing shoes, did you?" asked Sam, turning to Peter and Nathan. Peter and Nathan shook their heads.

"I didn't either," said Albert, "but I didn't ask him."

"Well, he was wearing shoes when the nurse carried him upstairs," said Victoria. "I saw his foot sticking out from under the blanket. And why was the nurse so interested in Albert?" she asked, looking at Albert who was gazing up at the darkened window and stepping backwards to get a better view.

"I expect she enjoyed talking to him. I expect she thought he was a very intelligent boy," said Akela defensively, as Albert tripped over the brick border surrounding the flower beds and crashed into a rosebush.

"I thought there was something weird about her," said Victoria.

"I think there's something strange about both of them," said Sam.

"Nonsense," said Akela briskly. "There's nothing strange about someone wanting to talk to Albert." He bent down to help Albert up. "And there's nothing strange about wearing shoes. Even if you don't walk in them," he added. "Now—" he glanced up at the sky — "let's get back before it starts raining again. Mr and Mrs Webb will begin to think we've got lost. This way, Albert," he said gently, as Albert started walking in the opposite direction to everyone else.

The children followed Akela, who had a flashlight, through the darkness towards the camp.

"I still think there's something suspicious about Mr Smith and his nurse," Sam whispered to Nathan and Peter, as they waited for Albert, who had tripped again, to pick himself up.

"So do I," hissed Victoria, who was stumbling behind Sam and overheard him.

"Come along, children," Akela interrupted, swinging the flashlight round at them. "We're nearly there."

They could see the lighted kitchen and hear the clatter of mugs.

"Good," said Akela, as they entered the campsite, "just in time for hot chocolate."

Skip and the rest of the children were crowded into the kitchen, noisily discussing Mr Smith with Mr and Mrs Webb.

Mr and Mrs Webb smiled proudly when Victoria came into the kitchen.

"We hear you've been performing miracles," Mrs Webb cried. "Isn't it wonderful?"

Sam, Peter and Nathan, who were standing behind Victoria as she opened her mouth to speak, felt themselves knocked aside by Albert, who tripped over the kitchen doorway and landed face down in front of Skip.

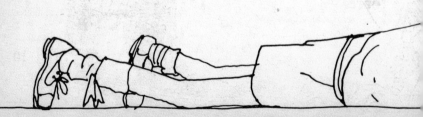

Victoria, who had closed her mouth until the twins' laughter died down, opened it again.

But it was Albert who spoke first. "The wellingtons," he gasped, gazing at Skip's boots.

"What's wrong with them?" Skip asked in surprise, looking down at his feet.

"Those wellingtons," said Albert dramatically, "are the wellingtons that pushed me into the stream."

Everyone stared at Skip's feet.

"Don't be silly, Albert," said Skip impatiently, "those wellingtons belong to Miss Hylyard."

"Are you sure?" Mrs Webb asked. She shook her head slowly. "Because they look awfully like the wellingtons that Mr Smith's nurse was wearing this afternoon."

12
Footprints!

Albert didn't sleep very well that night, even though Skip and Akela had assured him that there must be hundreds of pairs of boots like the pair Skip had borrowed and there was no reason for Mr Smith's nurse to push him into the stream, especially as she seemed to have taken a liking to him.

Sam, Nathan and Peter hadn't slept very well either.

They still thought there was something decidedly odd about Mr Smith and his nurse, in spite of the grown-ups agreeing that shock had caused Mr Smith suddenly to be able to walk and talk again. After breakfast, when Skip had asked if someone would like to return the wellingtons to Miss Hylyard, they volunteered, hoping to have another look at the couple.

Akela said that as all three wanted to go, they might as well return the pans Miss Hylyard had lent them, because they would have to start packing in the afternoon, and as they were having a cold lunch, the pans wouldn't be needed.

"And we don't want anything left behind this time," said Akela, noticing the two statues in the hollow tree. He was remembering the last time they were camping, and how astonished the twins seemed when Albert's rucksack, which had mysteriously disappeared, just as mysteriously reappeared on the top branches of the tree when they were about to leave. "I think, Albert," he continued, "that you'd better pack your statue away now, so you don't forget it. Sam, you'd better pack yours too," he added.

Sam, who was anxious to get to Miss Hylyard's, popped it into his pocket, to pack later. Then he, Peter and Nathan set off for the house.

Miss Hylyard was in the garden, holding a plant pot, when they arrived. "Good morning, boys," she greeted them, as they placed the wellingtons and the pans in the hallway. "You're up bright and early. My guests are having a little lie-in," she added, "so I thought I'd potter about in the garden and enjoy the sunshine. We did enjoy ourselves last night," she continued. "I'm afraid we stayed up rather late though, playing cards. And then of course there was that excellent horror film on at midnight.

"Still," she continued, "at least Mr Smith's nurse went to bed fairly early, which was just as well, as she was up at the crack of dawn for an early morning walk. Then they left," she explained. "They had to catch the early train to London." She frowned. "Although I'm not altogether certain that there is an early train on Sundays. I do hope they manage." She sighed. "It's quite a long walk to the station, particularly pushing a cumbersome wheelchair."

"Wasn't Mr Smith walking?" asked Sam.

Miss Hylyard looked at him in surprise.

"But, my dear," she said, "the poor man is

paralysed. He couldn't possibly walk. The nurse has to carry him everywhere when he's not in his wheelchair. Why, only this morning after her walk she carried him downstairs. I suppose that is why she has such highly developed muscles," she added, glancing at her watch. "Goodness," she exclaimed, "doesn't time fly? I must try and get this plant repotted before breakfast. Tell Skip and Akela I'll pop over after lunch to say good-bye."

Then before Sam could speak again, she thanked them for returning the wellingtons and pans, and walked away.

They took the longer way back, as they wanted to talk about Mr Smith and his nurse. "It's funny," said Sam, "but I'm absolutely certain it was Mr Smith I saw last night."

"But why would he pretend he couldn't walk?" asked Peter.

"I wonder if he was pretending he couldn't talk too," Sam said thoughtfully.

"But that's crazy!" Nathan objected.

Sam shrugged. "So many crazy things have happened," he said, "one more doesn't make much difference. Talking of crazy things," he gasped, stopping in his tracks. "Look!"

In front of them, partially hidden in a clump of trees, was a wheelchair.

"Blimey," whispered Peter.

"Come on," said Sam, pulling the two boys along with him. "Let's have a look at it."

The boys ran to the wheelchair and stared at it in silence.

Nathan was the first to speak. "Do you think they've gone for a swim?" he asked uncertainly. The cover of the wheelchair had been thrown back, and a pile of crumpled clothes lay on top of it.

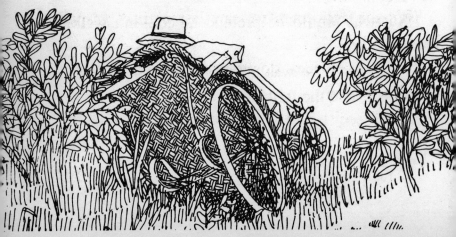

"We'll soon find out," said Sam, pointing at the trail of footprints embedded in the soft earth.

"They seem to be heading towards the camp," said Peter.

"One thing is certain." Sam frowned. "They definitely don't lead to the station." He looked at Peter and Nathan. "Well," he said, "what are we waiting for?"

The boys ran forward, down the slope that led to the campsite.

"Wait," cried Sam, throwing his arms out to prevent Nathan and Peter from going any farther.

They looked down at the clearing in disbelief.

They could still see the trail of footprints leading to the tents, and where the trail ended, two policemen stood, one big, the other small.

"It's the policemen we saw last night," gasped Nathan.

"What were they doing with the wheelchair?" exclaimed Peter.

"Sssh!" whispered Sam, straining to hear what the

policemen were saying to Skip and Akela.

He couldn't hear what the policemen were saying, but he did hear what the excited figure that ran into the clearing said.

"Come quickly, come quickly," Miss Hylyard cried, as she tugged at the policemen's sleeves. "The potting shed."

Sam whistled. "After them," he shouted, as the policemen hesitated, then followed Miss Hylyard.

"But why?" asked Peter and Nathan in astonishment.

"To find out what they're up to," yelled Sam, zigzagging through the trees as they raced after the blue-coated figures.

"Don't you realize? They're not the policemen we saw last night!" He paused for breath. "It's Mr Smith and his nurse!"

13
The Potting Shed

"Don't let them see us," Sam whispered, as they peered through the window of the potting shed.

Nathan and Peter could hardly recognize the nurse without the wig and make-up, and they certainly couldn't recognize Mr Smith because he had been covered up with blankets the last time they saw him.

The two men were glancing furtively round the room, while Miss Hylyard, who seemed quite excited, pointed at a pile of boxes in a corner.

"Hey!" gasped Nathan. "What are they doing?"

The boys' eyes widened as the bigger of the two men crept up behind Miss Hylyard with a large handkerchief.

"They're going to gag her!" Sam yelled, wrenching the potting-shed door open.

The boys dived at the big man's feet. The smaller

man grabbed Miss Hylyard, who had spun round in surprise, and pulling the handkerchief out of the big man's hand, wrapped it round her mouth, stifling her cry of alarm.

The big man shook the leg that Nathan was clinging to. Then, as Nathan spun across the room, he picked Sam up by the scruff of his neck, and shook the other leg. Sam gulped, as Peter went spinning across the room too.

Nathan had already been gagged by his own neckerchief, and now it looked as though it was Peter's turn.

"I recognize you, sir," the big man rumbled, sticking his face next to Sam's. "I have reason to believe, sir, that you have in your possession a little bauble, sir." He paused. "A statue to be precise, sir. Now—" he glanced around the room again—"as time is precious, it would save us the inconvenience of impersonating police officers who have been asked to retrieve stolen property if you were to tell us where

it is. It would also save Mustapha here the unpleasantness of persuading you to tell us." He nodded at the small man, who had tied up the gagged bodies with twine, and was glancing round the room too, making strange clicking noises with his tongue, as he nervously fingered an evil-looking dagger.

The big man laughed, making the hair on the back of Sam's head stand on end. "Unpleasant for you, sir, you understand," he added, "not for Mustapha. I might add, sir," he continued, "that another person was rather reluctant to part with it too." He sighed, and shook his head. "He needed a little persuading, sir, before he would tell us that the statue was hidden in the litter bin." He sighed again. "The poor man met with a most unfortunate accident afterwards."

He winked at Mustapha, who was still making peculiar noises and didn't seem to notice. "I searched for it, sir, and could only assume when I saw your bus departing from the very spot that one of you young gentlemen must have found it. You can imagine, sir, my disappointment when, to coin a phrase, I thought I had it in my pocket."

Sam, who had just remembered that the statue was in his pocket, instinctively put his hand there. The big man, noticing the movement, pushed Sam's hand away, reached into the pocket, and tugged at the statue. The statue, which had caught on the lining of the pocket, slipped from his grasp and fell down into an empty strawberry pot.

The big man dropped Sam and shouted at Mustapha, who hurriedly gagged Sam too.

The big man was trying to force his hand into the strawberry pot to get the statue, but his hand was too large. Picking up the pot, he made for the open door.

Mustapha, who had just finished tying up Sam, turned, and saw him. He shrieked, and lunged at the big man. The two men struggled violently with the pot, then suddenly Mustapha slid to the floor, his eyes closed.

The big man clutched the strawberry pot in the crook of his arm, and pointed at a pot that was by the door.

"That, sir," he said, looking at the leaves, then glancing at Sam, "is, I believe, an aspidistra!" His big frame shook with laughter. "How very appropriate, sir," he chuckled, "how very appropriate." Then still shaking with laughter, he closed the door and disappeared.

Miss Hylyard, who had seemed quite agitated throughout the proceedings, seemed even more agitated as she made muffled noises at the boys, who were quite bewildered by the big man's words.

The boys were helpless. They were bound so tightly they could hardly move, and gazed forlornly at Mustapha's knife, which lay tantalizingly out of reach next to Mustapha's senseless body.

Suddenly the door flew open.

"There you are," said Victoria accusingly. "I've been looking everywhere for you . . ." her voice

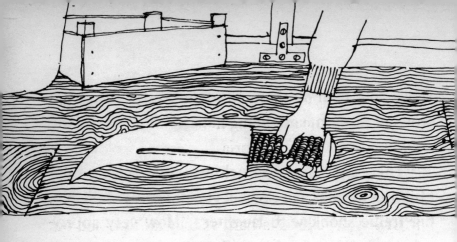

trailed off as she gazed at the trussed bodies, then at
Mustapha, and then at the knife.

"Crumbs," she exclaimed, "what happened?"

She picked up the knife and cut the twine that
bound Miss Hylyard's wrists and ankles.

"I'll tell you later, dear," Miss Hylyard gasped,
having torn the handkerchief from her mouth. "First
free the boys," she added urgently. "We must get
out of here immediately."

"Why?" asked Victoria, looking at Mustapha's
unconscious body, as she cut Nathan, Sam and
Peter free. "You're not worried about him being in
here, are you?"

"No, I'm not worried about him," Miss Hylyard

replied, as the boys jumped to their feet. "But I am worried about the asp being in here."

"The what?" said Victoria.

"The asp," Miss Hylyard repeated, pushing the children towards the door. "The poisonous snake."

"Crikey," yelled Nathan, as they all tumbled out of the doorway.

"I suppose," gasped Sam, jerking his head towards Mustapha, "that we ought to get him out before the asp gets him."

They dragged the man out of the shed, and closed the door.

"I think," said Miss Hylyard, lifting one of Mustapha's limp arms and studying the two tiny punctures in the skin, "that the asp has already got him."

14
Deductions

Miss Hylyard rushed back to the house to telephone the police, after asking the children to get everyone to meet her there, just in case the snake had slipped unnoticed out of the shed and was roaming the grounds.

Skip and Akela couldn't make any sense of the garbled message, but allowed themselves to be dragged towards the house by the four excited children.

Mr and Mrs Webb, who were quite concerned about the state Victoria was in, ran after them with the rest of the children.

"What on earth is going on?" Akela asked, as the four children hustled everyone into the house.

Miss Hylyard's guests, who had had only a garbled message too, were all talking at once. Percy the parrot sat on the chandelier squawking, while Miss

Hylyard stood in the hall, chattering excitedly on the telephone.

"We keep trying to tell you," Victoria shouted, stamping her feet in frustration, "but you won't listen. There's a dead man outside the potting shed, and a live snake inside it."

Everyone gasped and fell silent.

"And Mr Smith and his nurse," said Nathan quickly, taking advantage of the silence, "were the policemen."

"Only they weren't real policemen," Peter broke in, "and they weren't really Mr Smith and his nurse." He looked round at the confused faces. "Oh, you tell them, Sam," he finished.

Everyone listened open-mouthed as Sam explained what had happened.

"Can you believe it?" exclaimed Akela, when Sam had finished. "They must have wanted that statue very badly."

Skip nodded. "They certainly went to a lot of bother to get it," he said.

"It must have been them who wrecked the tents in the first place," said Victoria, as the twins looked accusingly at Skip, and Miss Hylyard's guests looked rather confused.

"Yes," said Sam thoughtfully, "and that white figure in the woods *was* the nurse, or rather, the big man," he corrected himself. "He must have been keeping watch to make sure no one disturbed Mr Smith, I mean Mustapha, while he searched for the statue. That owl cry must have been a warning that Mrs Webb was heading for the tents."

"And Albert's broken model," cried Nathan. "Don't you remember, Victoria? We saw them near the camp the day it was broken. You thought the nurse was a ghost, remember?"

"They probably smashed it when they realized it was only a clay copy," Akela murmured.

"And I bet the nurse, I mean the big man," said Peter, "did push Albert into the stream."

Skip nodded, smiling weakly at the twins, who

were gazing at him in an even more accusing way. "He was probably trying to get Albert's other model, just in case it was the real one, and when Albert grabbed it, suspecting that someone was behind him, the big man pushed him into the stream, so that Albert wouldn't get the chance to see who it was."

Miss Hylyard's guests, who had been trying very hard to get the drift of the conversation, looked totally baffled when Victoria spoke again.

"Ah," she exclaimed, "that's why the nurse was so keen to talk to Albert. He wanted to find out where Sam's statue was. I knew there must be a reason for him wanting to talk to Albert," she finished triumphantly.

"I suppose disguising themselves as policemen was the last resort," said Akela, "as Albert didn't tell them where the statue was. It was fortunate for them that the policemen left their uniforms to dry last night. They told us they were substituting for the policemen we met last night," he explained to

Nathan, Peter and Sam. "I thought it was a bit odd that they weren't wearing their helmets," he added.

"And then they were interrupted by Miss Hylyard," said Skip, "who asked them to go urgently to the potting shed with her—"

"Which they didn't seem too keen on," interrupted Akela, "but I suppose they thought we'd begin to be suspicious of them if they didn't go, especially as Miss Hylyard was so insistent. So they told us they'd be back in a few minutes."

"To say they were policemen looking for stolen property," Sam murmured, remembering the big man's words.

"Stolen property meaning an ibis," agreed Skip.

"Which we would have given them, of course," said Akela.

"Except that I had it in my pocket." Sam sighed. "And I suppose they had to keep Miss Hylyard quiet so they could go back for the statue. That's why they bound and gagged her."

Akela nodded. "I'm sure they would want to get away as quickly as possible, before the real police turned up. Still," he added, "it was quite a clever idea dressing up as a frail old man and his nurse. No one would suspect them of anything." He smiled. "Except for Sam, Nathan and Peter."

"And me," Victoria protested.

"I wonder how the snake fits into the mystery," Skip commented, "because I have a nasty feeling there's a connection somewhere."

Miss Hylyard, who had just entered the room, overheard Skip.

"Oh, there is," she said grimly. "There most certainly is."

15
The Stranger

Miss Hylyard looked round at the expectant audience.

"I'm sorry I've been so long," she apologized, "but it took me quite a while to convince the police that I wasn't pulling their legs. However," she added, "they're on their way over." She paused, waiting for the hum of conversation to die down.

"Now. The snake connection." She took a deep breath. "It was like this. I decided to go to the potting shed this morning. In fact—" she nodded at Sam, Nathan and Peter—"just shortly after the boys came to return the wellingtons and pans. I had a plant that needed repotting." She laughed mirthlessly. "An aspidistra; which, as that dreadful man commented, seemed very appropriate in the circumstances.

"As I set the plant down in the shed," she

continued, "I noticed that the rosemary bush, which is next to the shed, was looking a bit bedraggled, so I went to examine it to see if it needed pruning. To my surprise I saw, hidden under its branches, a suitcase and what looked like a portable writing case. I thought," Miss Hylyard went on, "that I ought to look inside the writing case to see if there was a name or address of the person it belonged to, so that I could return it.

"I should have taken my gardening gloves off," she said, "because as I opened the writing case it slipped from my hand and fell to the ground. Something clicked, a lever I believe, and to my astonishment what I thought was the base of the box slid away, revealing a snake, which immediately wriggled out of the box and into the potting shed.

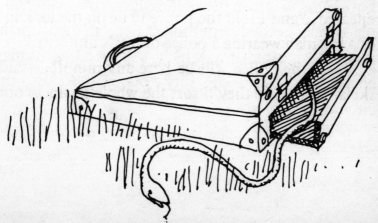

You can imagine how shocked I was.

"I recognized the snake as an asp," she explained, as everyone started talking excitedly, "as I had seen them on my trip to Egypt. Knowing how dangerous they were, I closed the potting-shed door and ran to tell you—" she looked at Skip and Akela—"but when I saw the policemen, I asked them to come instead. I didn't want to alarm the children by explaining why," she finished.

"They must have left the suitcase there so they could change into their own clothes once they'd got the statue," said Sam.

"Oh, dear," Miss Hylyard confessed, "I hadn't thought of that. That's exactly what the big man must have done, because the suitcase had gone when we escaped from the potting shed. Oh, dear," she repeated, "and I told the police to be on the lookout for a big man wearing a police officer's uniform."

"Well, the police will be here any minute," said Akela. "I'm sure they'll sort the whole business out in no time at all. They're bound to catch the big man," he added encouragingly as Miss Hylyard looked a bit dejected.

"I hope they catch the snake too," Skip murmured. "Still, at least it got one of the villains."

"And when the police catch the other villain, the whole thing will be settled," said Akela.

"I'm not so sure that there isn't another villain, though," said Sam, frowning. "The big man mentioned another man."

"The one who met with an unfortunate accident," Nathan added, as Miss Hylyard, hearing a knock on the door, hurried to open it.

The children, expecting to see the police, were surprised when a stranger, his ankle in plaster, limped into the room.

"I am sorry to intrude upon your gathering," he said, bowing low. "I am afraid," he apologized, glancing at his leg, "that I met with an unfortunate accident."

The children stared at each other open-mouthed. Then, before Akela could stop them, they dived at the stranger, and sent him flying to the floor.

"It's the bloke who works for the big man. Let's question him," Victoria cried, just as the door opened again, and two policemen rushed in.

"We've got the men looking for the rogue who tied you up," Sergeant Pattison shouted at Miss Hylyard, "and men searching for the snake." He stopped in horror when he noticed the stranger, who was looking rather dazed with children sitting on top of him and Miss Hylyard's guests surrounding him.

"Good heavens!" exclaimed Sergeant Pattison, rushing forward and pulling the protesting children off the man.

"But he's a crook," Victoria complained, trying to hang on to the man's foot. "We were making sure he didn't escape until you came."

"He's in league with the big man," Nathan added,

as the police officer who was with the sergeant lifted him off the man's back.

"And I bet if we use some persuasion he could tell us where the big man is," said Peter, as the policeman lifted him up too.

"Nonsense," snapped Sergeant Pattison, helping the man to his feet.

"Then who is he?" Victoria demanded as the shocked man blinked at them and straightened his tie.

"Professor Khan," said Sergeant Pattison, "Head of Cairo Museum in Egypt. He has just been explaining to us about the missing statue. He arrived at the station just after your telephone call," he added, turning to Miss Hylyard. "He has been sent by the Egyptian Government to try and track it down. With our help of course," he added proudly.

"Oh, dear," said Akela. "I think you children owe the professor an apology."

"It wasn't our fault," Victoria protested, after the

children had muttered apologies to Professor Khan. "He shouldn't have said he'd had an unfortunate accident."

"The professor," said Sergeant Pattison sternly, "slipped on the steps of the plane and hurt his ankle."

"Cairo Museum," Miss Hylyard murmured. "I was in Cairo myself several years ago."

"Professor Khan is the world-famous expert on Egyptian treasures," said Sergeant Pattison. "His picture has been in newspapers all over the world."

"You made mention of a big man," said the professor, who seemed to be coming out of his state of shock. "And a statue. Was the statue by any chance a statue of an Egyptian ibis?"

"Goodness," Miss Hylyard exclaimed, as the children nodded. "I didn't realize the fuss was all about an ibis. I didn't see the statue in the potting shed," she explained. "What an amazing coincidence. I sold a statue of an ibis to a foreign gentleman just a few days ago. I tried to tell him it was worth only a few shillings. I bought it in a bazaar in Cairo," she added, "but the gentleman thrust five pounds in my hand, and even though I protested that it was far too much, he seemed very happy with the deal."

"I am sure he was," said the professor grimly. "That statue is the only one of its kind in existence."

"Oh, but it's not," said Miss Hylyard. "There's another one upstairs in Percy's cage."

And to Miss Hylyard's surprise, the professor grabbed her by the arm and steered her towards the stairs.

The children, followed by Skip and Akela, Mr and Mrs Webb, the policemen, and Miss Hylyard's guests, raced after them.

16
The Egyptian Ibis

Nobody spoke as Miss Hylyard lifted the statue from the cage and handed it to the professor.

"Crumbs," whispered Sam, as the professor took a sharp knife from his pocket and scraped the black-coated statue.

A brilliant red ruby glowed through the coating.

"Crikey," muttered Victoria, as he scraped again, revealing a huge sparkling diamond that formed an eye.

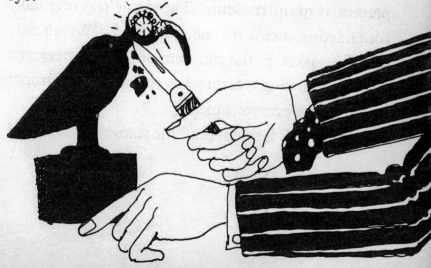

"The Egyptian ibis." The professor sighed, putting the knife back in his pocket. "At last, after all these years! Madam," he said, bowing to Miss Hylyard, who was so shocked she had to sit down on the bed, "the Egyptian Government is indebted to you for retrieving our country's most treasured possession."

"Then what is the statue that the big man has?" asked Sam in a dazed voice.

"A fake," said the professor. "This is the genuine Egyptian ibis. We've been searching for it for ten years." He stroked the statue dreamily. "It was stolen from a pharaoh's tomb thousands of years ago," he explained. "Eventually it was found and presented to the museum. The statue was originally contained in a casket," he continued. "We already had the casket in the museum and were overjoyed when the missing treasure was restored to its proper container for everyone to see.

"However," he went on, "the statue was removed

from the container ten years ago, and vanished without a trace. There is a legend," he added, "that a curse would fall on anyone who prevented the statue from lying in its proper container, and that the mummy, who had guarded the treasure in the tomb, would appear to such a person, who would then meet an untimely end by poison."

"Of course," Akela interrupted, turning to Miss Hylyard, who was still speechless, "Mr Smith, I mean Mustapha, must have thought Victoria was the mummy who had come to life."

"So," said the professor, "Mustapha was involved too. I suspected as much when Sergeant Pattison told me about the man who was bitten by a poisonous snake." He smiled at Victoria. "That was the unfortunate accident the big man told you about."

"So they killed him with the snake to get the statue off him," said Sam, "only they got the wrong statue."

"A very cunning thing to do," interrupted

Sergeant Pattison, "because everyone would think it was an accident."

The professor nodded. "Mustapha," he explained, "was a small-time crook in Cairo. He was also something of a snake charmer."

"His charm didn't work in the potting shed," Victoria observed. "It's his body outside it."

"Sergeant Pattison told me that Miss Hylyard had telephoned saying there was a body outside the potting shed," Professor Khan said. "So Mustapha was killed by his own snake."

"And he kept it concealed in an innocent-looking writing case!" said Miss Hylyard, who had just recovered her voice. She turned to her horrified guests. "And to think it was in this house!"

"That must be why Percy made such a noise when they came, and refused to go into his cage," said Sam. "As their rooms are next to yours, he must have smelled the snake."

"But how on earth did they know the statue was

there?" asked Miss Hylyard, bewildered.

The professor smiled again.

"They let someone else lead them to it," he said, taking a photograph from his pocket and showing it to Miss Hylyard.

"Why," said Miss Hylyard in surprise, "it's the gentleman that bought the statue from me."

"And the man the Egyptian Government has suspected for years," said the professor, "although they could prove nothing. Last month they had some information about a trip to England he was planning, and I was asked to follow him, to see if he could lead me to the statue."

"He was also the gentleman that met with the unfortunate accident," Sergeant Pattison added. "It seems that when he realized that the big man and Mustapha were on his trail, he hid the statue."

"And they persuaded him to tell them where he'd hidden it," said Sam, "but I found it first."

"The big man saw us leaving the village where the

rubbish basket was," said Peter. "He told us. That's why he followed us. He thought one of us must have found it."

"So they disguised themselves, and stayed at Miss Hylyard's to be near the Cub camp to search for it," murmured Akela.

"And after all that they ended up with a fake," said the professor, stroking the ibis.

"But how did anyone know the ibis was here?" Miss Hylyard asked the professor.

"My dear Miss Hylyard," the professor replied, "only you can explain that. Think back, to when you visited Cairo."

Miss Hylyard frowned. "It's such a long time ago," she said, "but I'll try to remember."

17
The Reward

"Well," said Miss Hylyard, looking round at everyone. "It was when my poor father was still alive. He was quite elderly, but had a wish to go to Cairo again, to see their wonderful museum. I decided to accompany him as he couldn't make the journey on his own. He insisted on going by boat as he didn't care for aeroplanes.

"The journey was very pleasant," she continued, "and the hotel was extremely comfortable. Well, one afternoon Father was taking his nap, and I decided to have a look around the bazaar, as it was our last day in Cairo. I saw some copies of the famous Egyptian ibis that we'd seen in the museum the day before, and I thought they would look quite nice on the mantel-piece. I remember buying them, and placing them on top of my shopping basket.

"I was on my way back to the hotel, when a gentleman rushed towards me in a state of great anxiety. He told me he had bought an ibis too, as a present for his wife, as it was their wedding anniversary the next day. His wife, apparently, had seen him, and was trying to catch up with him," Miss Hylyard broke off.

"His English was quite good," she explained.

148

"Anyway, he said he didn't want his wife to know about the gift, as it was to be a surprise. He asked me to keep it for him and he would collect it from me, at the same spot, at ten o'clock the next morning, which I agreed to do. He then rushed off so quickly I didn't have time to tell him that I'd just remembered that my boat left at nine o'clock. I ran after the gentleman to tell him, but he had disappeared."

Miss Hylyard paused for breath. "I was terribly concerned, as I didn't want to deprive the poor man's wife of her anniversary present, so I did the only thing I could think of. I went to the police station and gave them one of the statues. They were all the same," she explained, "except the one he'd bought was covered in nasty black stuff. I thought it would be much nicer for his wife to have a clean one, so she could see all the pretty bits of coloured glass on it. I gave the policeman one of mine and explained the situation.

"The policeman didn't seem terribly interested,

and said he doubted that the man would bother to collect it, as he could easily buy his wife another one. However, he took the statue and promised to look after it in case the man did turn up.

"I felt a little bit guilty when we got on the boat to return to England, thinking of the poor man waiting for me, but as Father said, I'd done the only thing I could. Father, I'm afraid, didn't care for the glass decorations on the statue and decided to paint it black to match the other one. When Father died, a friend gave me Percy. He looked a bit lonely on his own at night, so I put one of the statues in his cage to keep him company.

"I thought at the time," she added, frowning thoughtfully, "that it seemed a lot heavier than the other one. The rest you know," she finished. "I had to sell some bits and pieces to try and keep the place going, and sold the statue on the mantelpiece to the gentleman in the photograph."

"Who was the self-same man," said the professor, "as the man who gave it to you to look after in Cairo.

He stole the statue from the museum and painted it black to make it less conspicuous. He was being trailed by the police when he saw you and needed to get rid of the evidence. He was hoping, of course, to collect it from you the next day. But you didn't turn up.

"He spent the next ten years trying to find the ibis," the professor continued, shaking his head. "First he made inquiries at all the hotels in Cairo, and found out the names of all the English people who were staying there at the time. He has apparently made several trips to England, unknown to us, but his search was fruitless.

"It seems," he added, smiling at Miss Hylyard, "that your hotel proprietor had forgotten that you'd stayed there. It was only when he made inquiries at the shipping agents that he discovered another English couple had left Cairo at the particular time he was interested in. As he'd been to see all the other English people who had been in Cairo, he was sure that you must have it.

"The Egyptian authorities guessed what he was up to, and sent me to follow him, hoping he would lead me to the statue. They also knew that the big man was interested in the statue too, as he'd been making inquiries in Cairo as well. When Mustapha came to join him in England, they were fairly certain that the search for the statue was nearing an end."

"And after all that," Akela murmured, "they ended up with a fake."

"I know I shouldn't have taken five pounds for it," said Miss Hylyard guiltily, "but I did need the money."

"Well, my dear Miss Hylyard," said the professor gravely, "you will never need five pounds again. The Egyptian Government is giving a reward for the recovery of the statue. Ten per cent of the value of the ibis."

"How much is that?" asked Victoria.

"About half a million pounds," the professor replied.

18
Celebrations!

"Half a million pounds," echoed Miss Hylyard, as everyone gasped. "Oh—" she clasped her hands together — "it's a miracle."

"You wished for a miracle, and you got one," shouted Skip, throwing his beret in the air.

"And now my friends can stay forever." Miss Hylyard laughed, as her guests hugged one another in delight.

"And I won't have to sell the campsite after all, and all because Sam found a statue. Oh, it's wonderful." She sighed, smiling at the children. "And I'm going to install an amusement arcade for you," she went on breathlessly, "with lots of those wonderful Space Invader machines I've heard about, with tokens supplied of course, so you won't have to spend any money.

"And chocolate machines, and fizzy drink

machines, and oh! I mustn't forget, one of those marvellous jukeboxes that light up when you play a tune," she finished triumphantly. The children, who had been nodding enthusiastically, cheered, and Skip and Akela, who were beginning to look a tiny bit alarmed, clapped politely.

Miss Hylyard's guests, who were so excited they had started dancing round the room, persuaded the professor, beaming happily, to join in with them, and he did, in spite of his bad leg. Percy, who had been watching the proceedings from the chandelier, flew down and perched on top of the piano, waiting for Miss Hylyard to sit down and play.

Miss Lovatt went to fetch her piano accordion, while Mrs Earnshaw fished her mouth organ out of her handbag.

Sam, Nathan and Peter were asked to fetch the freshly made batch of cookies from the kitchen that Miss Hylyard had made for their journey home, and Victoria and Albert got the ginger beer from the cellar. Even the twins helped the younger Cubs to bring the glasses in, while two of Miss Hylyard's guests made mountains of chicken and mayonnaise sandwiches.

They all sang at the top of their voices at the impromptu party, and Sergeant Pattison and the policeman were very disappointed when the telephone rang, asking them to join the hunt for the big man, who still hadn't been found, and the snake, which hadn't been found either.

Their places were soon taken by the two policemen who had come for their uniforms. They listened in amazement as Sam, Peter, Nathan and Victoria told them what had happened.

The news of the discovery of the ibis soon leaked out, as Mr Underwood, one of Miss Hylyard's guests, had telephoned the local newspaper. To the children's and the guests' delight, the house was invaded by television, newspaper and radio reporters.

All the children were interviewed and told they would appear on TV on the six o'clock news. As the smaller children were anxious to get home and watch it with their parents, Akela said they'd better be heading back to London.

Albert insisted on giving Miss Hylyard his copy of the ibis to put in Percy's cage, and blushed happily when Professor Khan admired it.

Then they all said good-bye to Miss Hylyard, her guests, the off-duty policemen and Professor Khan, promising to return to the campsite soon.

"What a weekend," said Akela, after he, Skip and Mr Webb had cleared up and loaded the luggage on to the bus.

"It certainly was," agreed Skip, as the rest of the children sat on the bus waiting for Albert, who was tying his shoelaces, to get on.

"It was fantastic," murmured Victoria, who had decided to go back with the boys, after saying good-bye to her parents.

"I can't wait to come camping again," said Peter, thinking of the chocolate machines.

"Neither can I," agreed Nathan, thinking of Space Invaders, as Albert stumbled on to the bus and sat down in front of the twins.

"I was beginning to think the weekend was going to be disastrous," Skip admitted. "But it all turned out well in the end."

"I must say it's absolutely marvellous that Miss Hylyard doesn't have to sell the house," Akela said, "and that the statue is going back to where it belongs."

Sam, who was sitting quietly, suddenly spoke.

"I've been thinking," he said, frowning thoughtfully, "about the curse of the mummy's tomb. The curse said that anyone who tried to prevent the ibis from lying in its proper container would meet an untimely death from poison."

"But the two men who died were bitten by a snake," Victoria objected, "and anyway, they stole a fake statue."

"Yes," said Sam slowly, "but they meant to steal the real one. And an asp is a poisonous snake, so they did die from poison."

The children fidgeted uncomfortably.

"Oh, it's just a superstition," said Akela uneasily, as Skip turned on the radio to hear the road conditions. "The big man tried to get the ibis, and he seems to have got away."

Skip, who had turned up the radio as the children were all talking at once, shouted and interrupted them.

"Hey, listen to this," he yelled, turning up the radio still more.

Even the twins fell silent at the unexpected volume.

"We repeat our special news flash," the voice crackled through the bus. "Police at London airport are puzzled by the discovery of an unidentified body found in the airport lounge. The man," the voice continued, "who was clutching a strawberry pot, appears to be the victim of a deadly snake bite, as an asp was discovered curled around a worthless statue inside the pot."